Copyright © Troy Brown, Brown Digital Media 2020

Published by Troy Brown

All rights reserved. No part of this book may be reproduced or transmitted in any form or by any means, electronic or mechanical, including photocopy, recording, or by any information storage and retrieval system, without permission in writing from the author.

Written by Troy Brown
Illustrated by Troy Brown

Published in the United States of America

Library of Congress Cataloging-in-Publication-Data

Can I Touch Your Hair ?

ISBN- 978-0-578-82012-5

I dedicate this book to my darling niece Zaria Brown, a.k.a "Baby Shark," a.k.a "Sharkie," a.k.a "Barkie." May you always find your inner strength to overcome any obstacle. Your differences are your greatest super power. "You is kind, you is smart, you is important."

Love, Uncle Troy

There once was a girl with big curly hair.

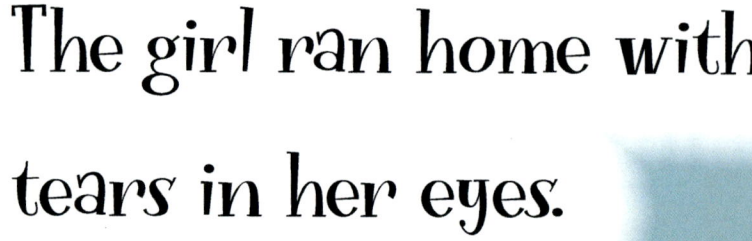

The girl ran home with tears in her eyes.

Hold your head high my child for your hair is your crown, every curl has a story so never look down.

You can still be my friend but, you may not touch my hair.

So when they go low, you continue to go higher!

Made in the USA
Monee, IL
08 August 2021